Zach stands Up

William Mulcahy

illustrated by
Darren McKee

free spirit
PUBLISHING®

Library of Congress Cataloging-in-Publication Data
Names: Mulcahy, William, author. | McKee, Darren, illustrator.
Title: Zach stands up / William Mulcahy ; illustrated by Darren McKee.
Description: Minneapolis : Free Spirit Publishing Inc., 2018. | Series: Zach rules
Identifiers: LCCN 2017041841 (print) | LCCN 2018011514 (ebook) | ISBN 9781631982941 (Web PDF) | ISBN 9781631982958 (ePub) |
    ISBN 9781631982934 (hardcover) | ISBN 1631982931 (hardcover)
Subjects: LCSH: Bullying—Prevention—Juvenile literature.
Classification: LCC BF637.B85 (ebook) | LCC BF637.B85 M845 2018 (print) | DDC 302.34/3—dc23
LC record available at https://lccn.loc.gov/2017041841

Reading Level Grade 2; Interest Level Ages 5–8;
Fountas & Pinnell Guided Reading Level K

Edited by Eric Braun
Cover and interior design by Tasha Kenyon

10 9 8 7 6 5 4 3 2 1
Printed in the United States of America
B10950318

Free Spirit Publishing Inc.
6325 Sandburg Road, Suite 100
Minneapolis, MN 55427-3674
(612) 338-2068
help4kids@freespirit.com
www.freespirit.com

SUSTAINABLE FORESTRY INITIATIVE
Certified Chain of Custody
Promoting Sustainable Forestry
www.sfiprogram.org
SFI-01268

SFI label applies to the text stock

Free Spirit offers competitive pricing.
Contact edsales@freespirit.com for pricing information on multiple quantity purchases.

Dedication

To Shannon, love Dad

Acknowledgments

Special thanks to Eric Braun, Margie Lisovskis, and the rest of the folks at Free Spirit Publishing for continuing to stand so strongly behind Zach and for coming up with the idea for this book.

Thank you to Robert Dewitt Thompson and Larry Gierach for some important discussions on bullying prevention.

Thank you to my wife Melissa for your incredible support and our extraordinary children.

And to those people who make great differences in our world by spreading messages of peace, understanding, and courage as upstanders, thank you for your inspiration!

Zach was eating lunch with Jaden, a popular kid from his soccer team. Roxy was there, too. Zach wanted Sonya to join them. But Roxy shook her head.

"You can't sit with us," Roxy said.

Sonya's smile turned down. "Why not?"

Jaden said, "It's reserved for people who don't smell."

"I don't smell!" Sonya said. "And I can sit wherever I want!"

Roxy waved a hand in front of her face. "Not here, you can't—P.U.!"

Zach didn't know what to do as he watched Sonya walk away. For the rest of lunch, he sat in silence while Sonya ate alone.

Zach was still upset in class that afternoon. He couldn't stop thinking about what Jaden and Roxy did to Sonya. He knew he should have stuck up for his friend, but he was too scared. Everyone was watching.

Zach got so distracted that he couldn't keep his mind on schoolwork. When Ms. Rosamond asked him to point to the dorsal fin on the board, he didn't know what she was talking about. He was totally lost.

After school, Zach sat on the bus waiting to go home. When Sonya came down the aisle, Roxy stuck her foot out, and Sonya tripped. Everyone laughed—everyone except Zach.

He scooted over to make room for Sonya on the seat. But she walked past him to the back.

At home, Zach was so upset he threw his backpack down the hall.

"Hey!" his brother said. The sight of Alex playing sheriff made Zach smile in spite of his bad mood.

"Sorry, Alex," Zach said. "I had a bad day." He told Alex what happened to Sonya. "The worst thing is, I didn't do anything to help her. I didn't know what to do."

"You should have dumped milk on their heads," Alex said.

Zach laughed, but he knew that wouldn't solve anything. "I'd just get in trouble," he said.

"It stinks to get picked on," Alex said. "These two kids used to steal my crackers at snack time. And they told everyone I was a crybaby. It made me so mad."

"What made them stop?" Zach asked.

Alex thought for a minute. "It got better after Caleb came over and talked to me. I *was* kind of crying. Caleb asked if I was okay."

Zach said, "When we talked about bullying in class, Ms. Rosamond said it's important to speak up when you see bullying happen. Just speaking up can make it stop a lot of the time."

"It felt good he was on my side," Alex said.

"What happened next?" Zach asked.

"We took off. Caleb and I went outside. I was glad to get out of there."

"I would take off, too," Zach said. "Who wants to hang around where kids are being mean?"

"I know," Alex said. "I was still pretty mad. Caleb asked me what happened, and I told him how they had been picking on me. I felt a lot better after I told him about it."

"Caleb sounds like a good friend," Zach said. "He's a good listener, just like Mom. My teacher Ms. Rosamund calls it active listening when someone asks questions and lets you know they understand."

Alex said, "Caleb said we should tell our teacher what happened. I didn't want to tattle, but we told him anyway. Mr. Gomez said it was good that we did."

Zach remembered Ms. Rosamond saying the same thing about reporting bullying. It is not tattling. It's keeping someone safe.

"The best part of all is that Caleb and I are friends now," Alex said.

Zach agreed, that was pretty cool.

Zach looked at the toy badge on Alex's costume. "I have an idea," he said.

12

The boys ran to the kitchen, where Zach grabbed a sheet of paper and a marker. He drew a star just like Alex's badge.

"The star has five points," Zach said. "The top point is the title: Stand Up to Bullying. The other four points can show the four things that Caleb did to stand up for you."

Zach wrote each of the things Caleb did next to a point on the star. Those things matched ideas that Zach had learned from Ms. Rosamond.

Stand Up to Bullying

Speak up—talk to the person being bullied.

Take off—get the person away from the bullying.

Actively listen—let the person talk about what happened.

Report—tell an adult what happened.

"The first letters of the steps spell STAR!" Alex said.

The next morning, Zach put his stand-up-to-bullying drawing in his backpack. He hoped that Jaden and Roxy would forget about being mean to Sonya today. Then he wouldn't have to do anything. But if they hurt her again, he would be ready. He would think about the **STAR**.

It happened after morning recess.

After Sonya hung up her coat, Roxy pulled it off the hook and let it fall to the floor. She and Jaden laughed as Sonya picked it up and hung it again. Again, Roxy dropped it.

"That smelly thing belongs on the floor," Roxy said.

Zach's heart began to thump hard. The other kids were watching. Roxy and Jaden were popular. Zach worried that everyone would take their side. But he knew he had to do something.

"Let me get that," Zach said to Sonya. He picked up her coat and hung it on the hook. "We better get to class."

"What do you care about her stupid coat?" Jaden asked.

"It's my friend's coat," Zach said. "I'm just helping her."

"That coat has stink germs," Jaden said. "That's why nobody likes Sonya-Stinkola."

"That's not true," Zach said. "Sonya has been my best friend ever since preschool—and she doesn't stink."

Another girl spoke up then. "I like Sonya, too," Charlene said. "We go fishing down at the creek in the summer."

"Who cares?" Roxy mumbled. But she didn't say anything else.

"Come on, let's take off," Zach said to Sonya.

They stopped in the hallway on the way to class. "Are you all right?" Zach asked.

Sonya took a deep breath. "I'm better now," she said. "I've tried to ignore those guys, but they kept on being mean to me. I told them to stop, but that didn't work either. I'm glad to know I have friends who care."

After school, Zach and Sonya told Ms. Rosamond about what happened. Zach showed Sonya and Ms. Rosamond his **Stand Up to Bullying STAR**.

"That's very cool!" Ms. Rosamond said. "It can be really scary to stand up to bullying. It's important to remember that you *can* do something."

"It feels good to help someone," Zach said. "But Ms. Rosamond?"

"What is it?"

"What happens now?" Zach wondered if Jaden and Roxy would be mean to Sonya again—or to him. He also wondered if Roxy and Jaden would be in trouble. Would any of them be friends again?

"I will talk with them," Ms. Rosamond said.

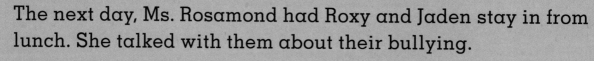

The next day, Ms. Rosamond had Roxy and Jaden stay in from lunch. She talked with them about their bullying.

"Roxy, do you remember how you felt when those girls spread mean rumors about you earlier in the year?"

"It felt terrible," Roxy said sadly.

"I remember that," Jaden said. "You were really upset."

"How do you think Sonya felt when you left her out and picked on her?" Ms. Rosamond asked.

"Also terrible," Roxy admitted. "I never thought about that."

"We just thought it was funny," Jaden said. "We didn't think about her feelings at all."

"Is there anything I can do to fix it?" Roxy asked.

"You can let Sonya know that you know you hurt her and you won't do it again," Ms. Rosamond suggested.

Later, at recess, Roxy went up to Sonya, looking friendly.

Sonya was nervous. What if it was a trick and Roxy was going to say something mean?

But Roxy said, "Sonya, I'm really sorry I was mean to you. I know it must have really hurt. I promise I won't act that way anymore. Will you play soccer with us?"

Sonya thought about it. Roxy seemed like she really meant it. "Okay," she said. "Let's play!"

When people don't say anything about bullying, they allow it to keep happening. When you need help standing up to bullying, you can use the **Stand Up to Bullying STAR**. **S**peak up by talking to people being bullied, and **T**ake off by helping them leave the area. Ask questions about how they are feeling, and **A**ctively listen to the answers. **R**eport what happened to an adult as soon as you can. It's important to support people who are bullied by continuing to talk with them and including them in the future. It takes a lot of courage to stand up to bullying. Remember, your decision to *do something* makes all the difference.

Helping Children Stand Up to Bullying

Bullying is a repeated pattern of hurtful behavior done by a person who has more power (physically or socially) than the person being targeted. Because of that inequity of power, many children are not equipped to deal with the emotional and social challenges that bullying presents. The situation can seem very scary and uncomfortable not only for targets but also for kids who witness bullying. But it's these witnesses, or bystanders, who often hold the most important power of all—the power to stop bullying. Studies show that the most effective thing a bystander can do is support the target of the bullying—by helping or being kind, not by directly confronting the aggressor. Thus, in order to help kids who are bullied and create environments where bullying is not tolerated, it is important to show children how to move beyond being a bystander to being an *upstander*, someone who stands up when they see bullying happen.

The **Stand Up to Bullying STAR** is a four-part process that gives children a specific plan for being an upstander that keeps everyone safe and helps them stay in charge of their thoughts, feelings, and behaviors. It helps them find the courage to include and support kids who are being bullied, help those kids get away from the bullying situation, and continue to encourage targeted kids by listening to them. It also includes perhaps the single best strategy for helping kids who are targets of bullying: getting support from an adult at school.

Kids are most successful standing up to bullying when families, schools, and communities work together to guide and coach them. Help kids by practicing the **Stand Up to Bullying STAR** with them.

The **Stand Up to Bullying STAR** has the power to:

- Increase self-esteem and self-worth
- Increase sense of self-efficacy
- Help children stand up to their fears
- Help them feel empowered
- Help kids realize that neither the bullied nor the bystander are to blame
- Restore self-respect
- Build confidence
- Increase a sense of empathy

Here is more information about the four parts of the **Stand Up to Bullying STAR** and some tips to help guide your child.

1. **Speak up.** The most important thing a child can do in the moment he or she witnesses bullying is choose *not* to do nothing. Doing nothing is allowing the bullying to continue. Instead, the upstander can actively intervene by talking to or adjoining with the person being bullied. Speaking up has the power to show kids who are mistreated that someone cares about them and seeks to understand what they are going through. Never underestimate the power of empathizing. A common misconception is that speaking up means verbally challenging the person who is doing the bullying. In fact, this type of challenging behavior can escalate the bullying situation and cause further harm. It can be helpful to try to distract the people who are mistreating others, to find a way to change the subject or shift the focus to something else.

2. **Take off.** In this step, the upstander helps the person being bullied get away from the situation. Make sure kids know that this is not "being chicken" or running away from the problem; rather, it is the wisest and safest action to take. It helps stop the bullying. Coach kids to ignore any verbal attacks the bullying person might make when they take off and to stick to their exit strategy.

3. **Actively listen.** Once safely away from the bullying situation, upstanders listen to the concerns of the child being bullied without judging. Ask questions, be attentive, and reflect back what the other person might be feeling. This type of listening builds trust, teamwork, and a sense of belonging. Compassionate listening also is a powerful way to acknowledge someone and often increases self-esteem. Make sure to provide spaces and time where children can talk and listen without fear of being overheard. Be a good model by practicing good listening yourself.

4. **Report.** In this step, children tell an adult. Be sure to establish a culture in which children know they will never get in trouble for coming forward to inform about bullying. It is hard enough to watch or be the target of bullying. We don't want to further traumatize kids by shaming them or disapproving of their having the courage to come forward. Bullying thrives when kids believe they can't tell an adult because they will be labeled a tattletale. This is one way those who bully maintain their power and control over others.

Upstanders can do a lot for those who are targeted by continuing to support them after the bullying incident is done and reported. They can include these children in activities; invite them to sit together at lunch, on the bus, and at other times; and continue to listen to them. Being an ally not only supports the person targeted but can also help prevent future bullying, since kids who are seen as lacking friends are often targeted.

A few other tips:

- Talk with kids about bullying—what it looks like, what it feels like, and what they can do about it. Kids as young as four years old can understand the general concept.

- Never blame the person being bullied or the bystander for the bullying.

- Listen to kids who are bullied, encourage them, and check back with them over time.

- Don't pass judgment by saying things like, "You should have . . ." Don't tell a target that the bullying would not have happened if he or she had acted differently, and never tell the child to stop tattling.

- One of the more prominent avenues for bullying, even for young children, is cyberbullying—bullying that takes place using electronic technology and platforms such as social media, text messages, chats, and websites. Limit electronics usage and monitor what your children do online.

- Just like kids who are targeted and kids who witness bullying, children who bully need support and education. Help them understand what bullying is, and emphasize that it is not okay. Have open and nonjudgmental discussions and teach empathy, social skills, and respect. Provide clear and meaningful consequences that fit the situation. At this age, that might mean timeouts or taking away privileges or activities for a short period. Avoid shaming, yelling, and overly punitive punishments like extended grounding. Praise children when they make progress. Of course, teach by example by avoiding violent behaviors and modeling positive discipline and compassion.

It can be hard to think about our children being involved in bullying in any role. But we can equip them to handle bullying when they inevitably experience it. Use the **Stand Up to Bullying STAR** to teach children how to protect themselves and others from bullying and help create a culture where bullying is not acceptable.

Download a printable copy of the Stand Up to Bullying STAR at www.freespirit.com/STAR.

About the Author

Bill Mulcahy is a licensed professional counselor and psychotherapist. He has served as the supervisor at Family Service of Waukesha and as a counselor at Stillwaters Cancer Support Center in Wisconsin, specializing in grief and cancer-related issues, and he has worked with children with special needs. Currently he works in private practice in Pewaukee, Wisconsin, and is the owner of Kids Cope Now, a program for providing books and tools to help kids better cope with life's difficulties. Bill's picture books include the Zach Rules series and *Zoey Goes to the Hospital*. He lives in Summit, Wisconsin, with four children, three stepchildren, and his wife Melissa in a home where life is never boring. His website is kidscopenow.com.

About the Illustrator

Darren McKee has illustrated books for many publishers over his 20-year career. When not working, he spends his time riding his bike, reading, drawing, and traveling. He lives in Dallas, Texas, with his wife Debbie.

More Great Books from Free Spirit

Zach Rules Series

by William Mulcahy, illustrated by Darren McKee

Zach struggles with social issues like getting along, persevering, handling frustrations, making mistakes, and other everyday problems typical of young kids. Each book in the Zach Rules series presents a single, simple storyline involving one such problem. As each story develops, Zach and readers learn straightforward tools for coping with their struggles and building stronger relationships now and in the future.

Each book: 32 pp., color illust., HC, 8¼" x 8¼", ages 5–8.

The Weird Series

by Erin Frankel, illustrated by Paula Heaphy • Each book: 48 pp., color illust., PB, 9½" x 8", ages 5–9.

Free downloadable
Leader's Guide
available at
freespirit.com/weird

Interested in purchasing multiple quantities and receiving volume discounts?
Contact edsales@freespirit.com or call 1.800.735.7323 and ask for Education Sales.

Many Free Spirit authors are available for speaking engagements, workshops, and keynotes.
Contact speakers@freespirit.com or call 1.800.735.7323.

For pricing information, to place an order, or to request a free catalog, contact:

free spirit PUBLISHING®

6325 Sandburg Road • Suite 100 • Minneapolis, MN 55427-3674
toll-free 800.735.7323 • local 612.338.2068 • fax 612.337.5050
help4kids@freespirit.com • www.freespirit.com